THE GOLDEN COMPASS™

THE GOLDEN MONKEY

and the

Duel of the Dæmons

NEW LINE CINEMA
A Time Warner Company

SCHOLASTIC INC.
New York Toronto London Auckland Sydney
Mexico City New Delhi Hong Kong Buenos Aires

ISBN-13: 978-0-545-05934-3
ISBN-10: 0-545-05934-8

12 11 10 9 8 7 6 5 4 3 2 1   8 9 10 11 12 13/0

Printed in the U.S.A.   01

This printing, February 2008

CHAPTER ONE

*T*he Golden Monkey blinked in amazement. Even he – who was used to sumptuous, extravagant surroundings – was stunned by the sheer beauty of this great hall.

The ceiling stretched so high into the shadows that it was impossible to tell where it ended. Expensive wood panelling covered the walls, while tall windows decorated with intricate oval leading allowed in enough mellow evening light to bathe the grand hall with a soft glow. Tables ran along the walls. Above them were larger-than-life portraits of distinguished scholars. These pictures were pretty dull in themselves, but their glittering golden frames would have made even the ugliest painting look like a masterpiece.

So *this* was what the inside of Jordan College looked like.

The long tables were laden with golden plates and crystal glassware and dozens upon dozens of flickering candles. The Golden Monkey could already smell the wonderful aroma of the evening's meal and guessed that the college servants waited for all the seats to be filled before serving.

Suddenly, he saw that Mrs Coulter was making her way towards the head table. And quite right too – she was *very* important, after all. Mrs Coulter was a major force within the Magisterium – the organization that controlled and directed people's lives – and she had great power and influence. The Monkey was honoured to be her dæmon – a special part of her soul that existed outside of her body in the form of an animal. A single place remained at the table, next to a cross-looking young girl. The dæmon groaned to himself. He disliked children at the best of times.

But Mrs Coulter did not seem bothered by the prospect of spending the evening beside an annoying girl. Quite the opposite, in fact. Casting a sideways glance at Mrs Coulter, the Golden Monkey saw that she was wearing her most charming smile. He clung on to the silky fabric of her evening gown as the tall and very elegant woman slid into the empty seat.

'Lyra, my dear,' the Master of the college was saying to the girl. 'The Tutor of Metaphysics tells me that you missed your lesson again.' He took a deep breath. 'I know you do not always understand our wish to educate you, but sometimes you must do what others think best.'

'I disagree, Master,' said Mrs Coulter smoothly.

The crowded table of male scholars fell silent as she spoke and the Monkey couldn't help feeling immensely proud of her. Jordan College was one of the most prestigious seats of learning in Oxford, and its scholars were amongst the most accomplished in the world.

But no one had such a commanding and impressive presence as Mrs Coulter – and no one was as beautiful. It was hardly surprising that the scholars stopped conversing to listen to her speak.

'When I was a young woman of Lyra's age,' Mrs Coulter continued, 'I knew that no one could really, truly understand me – except of course my dæmon – and that it would be best if we were free to do as we pleased.'

She smiled at the girl, who stared back goggle-eyed.

The Golden Monkey tutted quietly. The child had *no* manners. As for the Master – well, he had stopped talking now too. Obviously, no one was used to having a woman with opinions around here.

'Who's she?' said a small voice. The softly spoken words were almost drowned out by the sound of clinking cutlery. It was the girl's dæmon talking – it had taken the form of a small, white cat.

The Golden Monkey shuddered. How unbearably *cute*. Children's dæmons changed almost constantly until they settled upon their final shape, so there was no excuse for the girl having so dull a companion. He prided himself on his sleek golden fur and quick mind. *He* was just the sort of dæmon that Mrs Coulter deserved – beautiful and intelligent, just like her.

'Dunno,' the girl replied in an undertone. 'But she shut up the Master, all right.'

The Master himself spoke. 'Mrs Coulter, this is our Lyra.' He turned to the girl. 'Lyra, this is Mrs Coulter. A ... friend of the college.'

The Golden Monkey chuckled to himself, taking care to keep the mirth from showing in his expression. A friend of the college? Well, that was one way of putting it.

***

Much, much later, long after the meal was finished and the dishes and cutlery had been cleared away, a few people still remained in the great hall of Jordan College. Mrs Coulter and Lyra were engrossed in a deep conversation, much to the Golden Monkey's disgust. Wasn't there anyone more worthwhile for Mrs Coulter to talk to around here than a child?

'...an' I was a baby when my parents died in an airship accident,' said Lyra, who had been telling the story of her life. Thankfully, it hadn't taken long. 'So my Uncle Asriel left me here with the scholars.'

'What a fascinating story,' said Mrs Coulter in a silken voice that betrayed no emotion. 'I've met Lord Asriel. It was at the Royal Arctic Institute. We'd discussed the political structure of the Ice Bears of Svalbard.'

Lyra looked amazed. 'You've seen an Ice Bear?' she breathed.

'Of course,' replied Mrs Coulter. 'Though in the North, as you know, they call them Panserbjørne.' She bent her head nearer to Lyra's, as if about to share a great secret. 'As a matter of fact, I've had an audience with the bear-king himself, Ragnar Sturlusson. And I'll tell you something I probably shouldn't...'

Lyra leaned closer. She seemed utterly entranced by the attention of the beautiful woman. The Golden Monkey couldn't blame her. Mrs Coulter had bewitched many a soul during her lifetime.

'King Ragnar is *desperate* to have a dæmon of his own,' Mrs Coulter continued. 'Bears don't have them, you see. And Ragnar, who likes to think of himself as a *person*, will stop at nothing to get one.' She paused, allowing the words to sink in. 'You mustn't repeat that,' she added. 'I told you because I feel I can trust you.'

'Oh, I'd never—' said Lyra.

But Mrs Coulter cut off her protests at once. 'Do you know...' she began, as if a wonderful thought had suddenly occurred to her. 'I'm going back to the North very soon. And I shall need an assistant...' She looked closely at the girl, a smile hovering around her immaculately painted lips. 'Perhaps *you* should come along.'

Lyra's face lit up with excitement. 'Me?' she asked. 'Go to the North?'

The Golden Monkey looked at her closely. Was this child's every thought reflected in her face? Had she *never* learned caution? He watched as her dæmon popped his head from beneath the table and became a downy white ermine.

'You would have to work very hard with me in London to prepare,' Mrs Coulter went on. 'You'll have to learn mathematics and navigation and celestial geography.'

'Would *you* teach me?' asked Lyra eagerly. 'I wouldn't mind *that*, not at all.'

'Well then,' said Mrs Coulter. 'It's decided.' She paused and thought silently for a moment. 'But I had better get the Master's permission.' At once, she turned to the elderly scholar, who appeared engrossed in his thoughts. 'Master?'

He looked up warily.

'I wonder if I might borrow dear Lyra?' she said. 'Only for a while, of course.'

The Master did not seem in the slightest surprised by this, but he did appear concerned. He and Mrs Coulter shared an odd look.

'I'm not sure that would be consistent with Lord Asriel's wishes for her education,' said the Master. He was stony-faced with disapproval.

'Oh, let me deal with Asriel,' said Mrs Coulter brightly. 'You mustn't deny me this little thing, you really mustn't.'

Although her voice was utterly charming, the Master appeared threatened. 'Lyra, do you wish to go?' he asked, as if the child were the only one with the power to accept or reject such a gracious invitation.

'Yes, please!' she exclaimed.

The Master, appearing suddenly exhausted by the conversation, gave a small, reluctant nod.

Lyra clapped happily.

The Golden Monkey had ducked beneath

the table, where the girl's ermine was crouching in the darkness. They were both dæmons, each part of a human's soul, yet so different. The Monkey stretched out a small paw towards the ermine. If Mrs Coulter was making a new friend, then it was natural their dæmons should do the same. The Monkey smiled to himself as he stroked the dæmon's white fur.

The look of discomfort on the ermine's face was priceless.

CHAPTER TWO

*T*aking care never to stray too far from Mrs Coulter, the Golden Monkey scurried up and down the corridors. At every door, he stopped to listen. It wasn't long before he found what he was searching for. Quickly, he hid himself near the heavy, wooden door in the darkest shadows – and waited.

'You'll be glad when I'm gone,' said Lyra, her voice sounding clearly through the door. 'It'll be ever so much easier for you.'

'That's right,' said a woman's voice, trembling with emotion. Then she burst into tears.

A lone figure plodded along the corridor before stopping at the door and knocking softly. It was the Master of the college and in his hand was a small, leather satchel.

Inside the room, the tearful maid hugged Lyra tightly. Hearing the Master's knock, she reluctantly let the girl go, wiping the tears from her eyes as she opened the door.

'Could you stay by the door, Mrs Lonsdale?' the Master asked her. 'It's important that I know if I was followed.'

At this, the Golden Monkey shrank even further into the shadows, watching warily as the maid stationed herself at the door. It closed behind her with a loud click.

The Master spoke quietly, but the Monkey had very good hearing.

He heard every word.

'Lyra,' the ancient scholar said. 'Much as I should like to, I cannot prevent you from going with Mrs Coulter.'

'Oh,' replied Lyra. She sounded surprised – almost disappointed to have been robbed of the opportunity to argue. 'Can't you? Oh.'

Despite Lyra's excitement about going to London, part of her didn't want to leave Jordan

College. It was her home.

'As a man of considerable learning,' the Master continued, 'who has your best interests at heart, I would advise you against the trip. Would that do any good?' He was silent for a moment or two, as if waiting for her reply. 'I thought not. Then I will ask you a favour. A great and grave favour.'

The Master's words hung ominously in the air. Then he took a small, round object from his satchel and gave it to Lyra.

'What is this?' she asked.

The Golden Monkey seethed with curiosity, but even a creature as skilful as he couldn't see through a solid wooden door. Instead, he listened all the harder, desperate for clues as to what had changed hands.

'An alethiometer,' replied the Master, watching Lyra as she inspected the object. 'It was given to the college by Lord Asriel, many years ago. And now I am giving it to you. I feel you are meant to have it.'

'But what's it for?' asked the girl.

The Master's reply was cryptic – far too cryptic for the Monkey, who couldn't see the object that they were talking about.

'It tells the truth,' the older man said. 'Since Asriel left you in our care, child, we have always tried to acquaint you with the truth. But the secrets at the heart of things elude scholars and authorities. This lets you glimpse them as they are…' He paused, then hurried on, as if guessing her next question. 'But I am afraid I could not teach you how to use it, not if we had all the time in the world. The art is lost.'

There was a long silence before the Master spoke again. When he did, his voice was very solemn.

'Lyra, this is the great and grave favour,' he said. 'That you keep the alethiometer to yourself. It is of utmost importance – to yourself, to all of us, perhaps to all creation – that Mrs Coulter

does not know you have it. Do you understand me? Of the utmost importance. The utmost.' He paused before adding, 'Bless you, Lyra. Bless you. Keep your own counsel.'

The Golden Monkey listened with growing fascination. He didn't know what this alethiometer looked like, but he knew what it did. And, most important of all, he knew that the wizened old Master wanted to keep it secret from Mrs Coulter. One way or another, he would have to find out more about Lyra's mysterious new possession.

CHAPTER THREE

*I*t was time for Lyra to leave Oxford. Wearing a sensible coat for travelling, she was loitering in the great quad at the heart of Jordan College when Mrs Coulter and the Golden Monkey arrived at first light. The porters were making a great fuss of her as they made their farewells.

'Where's Roger?' was the first thing the girl said.

'Maybe he's working—' began her dæmon. By now, the little cat had been introduced as Pantalaimon, or Pan for short.

'He'll want to say goodbye!' cried Lyra passionately. She looked terribly upset.

Mrs Coulter was in a hurry. 'Lyra, are you ready, dear?' she asked, as soon as she arrived.

'There's someone missing...' explained Lyra. She looked around distractedly, as if expecting this someone to jump out from behind a plant pot or appear out of thin air.

Mrs Coulter wore a polite, but slightly strained smile. 'Who is Roger, dear?' she said.

'My friend,' said Lyra. 'He works in the kitchens—'

Suddenly, Mrs Coulter's expression hardened. 'Lyra, we must go now because the ferry's about to take off,' she said briskly. 'But you can write to Roger – tell him all about the journey. You can send him a photogram.'

'Yes... I suppose...' said Lyra. And reluctantly, she trudged towards the great Sky Ferry that hung above the ground like an oversized cloud.

In a matter of moments, they were on their way to London and to Mrs Coulter's home.

The Golden Monkey gazed out of the Sky Ferry window at the bustling metropolis below. London looked remarkably good from the sky. It spread beneath them, crammed with miniature versions of all the famous landmarks – the Houses of Parliament, Tower Bridge, Battersea Power Station and the Atomworks at Fulham. Elegant skyscrapers peppered

the skyline, while the Thames twisted this way and that through the great city. Glowering over it all was the vast building known as the Magisterial Seat.

The Sky Ferry floated onwards, heading for the huge aerodrome near the city's centre – its final destination. From here, they would make their way to Mrs Coulter's London residence.

Lyra and Pan were captivated by the view and Mrs Coulter smiled at their obvious wonder.

'Mrs Coulter?' asked Lyra, pointing to the vast building. 'What's that?'

'That is the Magisterial Seat, Lyra,' replied the elegant woman. 'The offices of the Magisterium.'

Lyra didn't appear at all satisfied by the wordy reply. 'What is the Magisterium *for*?' she insisted.

The woman laughed, her blonde hair swaying gently as she did so. 'You *have* been living in an ivory tower,' she said. 'The Magisterium is what people need. They keep things working by telling people what to do.'

Lyra still looked puzzled. 'But ... you told

the Master that you did whatever you pleased,' she said.

'Well...' Mrs Coulter wrinkled her beautiful brow thoughtfully.

The Golden Monkey knew that she was searching for just the right answer to keep the child satisfied.

'Some people know what's best for them, and some people don't,' the woman continued in a softer tone. 'Besides, they don't tell people what to do in a mean, petty way. They tell people what to do in a kindly way – to keep them out of danger. Like parents tell children what to do, or teachers tell their pupils.'

Silently, the Monkey applauded Mrs Coulter's clever way with words. Nevertheless, he was surprised to see that the girl looked a little unsure, before smiling at last. He realized that she perhaps wasn't quite as easily fooled as she appeared...

CHAPTER FOUR

*T*he Golden Monkey took for granted how luxurious Mrs Coulter's home was. But now, as he witnessed Lyra's gasp of amazement, he saw it again through her eyes.

Although the house was as grand as any Jordan College room, it was comfortable in a way that they were not. It was pretty and feminine – soft, flowing fabrics hung at each window, while a luxuriously thick swathe of scarlet carpeted the wide, curving staircase. The furnishings were simple, but elegant.

It was a marvellous place to live.

Mrs Coulter wasted no time in showing an awe-struck Lyra around the many, high-ceilinged rooms of her impressive house. Soon, they reached an upstairs corridor and came to a halt beside a closed door.

'This will be your room,' Mrs Coulter said. 'At least, if you like it.' And she pushed open the door to reveal a bedroom fit for a princess. It was white and pink, feminine and beautiful. It even had its own bathroom.

Lyra was speechless.

It was obvious to the Golden Monkey that it was unlike anything she'd ever seen before.

***

Later that evening, dressed in an exquisite nightgown, Lyra stepped cautiously over the threshold of her new bedroom. Everything was pretty and soft, especially the feather bed, which was impossibly plump and inviting. Pan flitted about the room, sniffing at first one perfect thing and then another and another.

Lyra smiled at her dæmon, took a breath and then launched herself into the very middle of her huge, new bed. Pantalaimon followed,

leaping as a cat, before metamorphosing into a songbird, which swooped through the air. He changed back into a cat at the last moment, landing with a soft *boing* beside Lyra. The two played happily together, giggling contentedly.

Then Lyra reached under her pillow, where she had hidden the alethiometer. Slowly, she slid the strange object from the small, leather satchel that the Master of Jordan College had used to carry the device.

Neither she nor the cat dæmon seemed to have the slightest idea that they were being spied on... Outside, in the corridor, the Golden Monkey leaned closer to the door, listening intently.

Inside the room, Lyra studied the unusual object. It looked like a compass.

A golden compass. The size of a large pocket watch, it fitted snugly into the palm of Lyra's hand. Tiny symbols – too tiny to

see from this distance – decorated the edge of the object, where numbers would usually appear on a watch. A needle swung round the compass's face, seemingly of its own accord, while there were dials to control who knew what.

'The needle keeps stopping at the same symbols,' Lyra was saying. 'The lady ... the lightning bolt ... and the baby. Then it goes back and does it again, see?' She showed the alethiometer to Pan, who peered at it closely.

'There are some hands too, like on a clock,' said her dæmon. 'But three of them...'

Lyra twiddled the dials. 'Oh! I can move them,' she exclaimed with delight.

Hidden behind the door, the Golden Monkey listened to the conversation with growing fascination. What was this mysterious device? It had three hands in addition to a needle. And these hands pointed to strange symbols. One thing was for certain – he would have to find a way to acquire the object.

'The Master said it told the truth,' whispered Pantalaimon. 'Ask it something.'

Lyra thought for a moment. Then it came to her. She would ask the alethiometer about Dust. This was something she'd heard spoken of at Jordan College. The scholars and her Uncle Asriel had talked about mysterious particles from space that Asriel had observed in the North – they'd called them Dust. It had interested her then and it interested her now.

She held the alethiometer at arm's length and spoke to it as if the object were really a very important person instead of a piece of metal filled with clockwork mechanisms. 'What's Dust?' she asked.

At once, the swinging needle came to a dead stop. Then it began to move again, going round and round and round.

'Now it's not stopping anywhere,' said Lyra, her words heavy with disappointment.

'What do you think makes the needle move?' Pantalaimon asked wonderingly.

Lyra thought before replying. 'I don't know,' she said. 'Maybe Uncle Asriel knows. Maybe we're supposed to take it to him...'

Outside the room, the Golden Monkey heard soft footsteps. He swivelled to see Mrs Coulter approaching. She gave him a meaningful look, and then knocked gently at the door. Together, they went in.

Quickly, Lyra squirrelled away the alethiometer under her pillow again.

'All washed and ready for bed?' asked Mrs Coulter brightly. 'You've had a long day. You must be sleepy.'

Lyra looked surprised by such attention.

She lay down dutifully and seemed taken aback when Mrs Coulter bent down to tuck the bedclothes around her.

'Has no one ever tucked you in?' the woman asked.

'Not if that's what you're doing, no,' muttered Lyra, looking most uncomfortable with the attention.

'I can't imagine,' said Mrs Coulter, almost to herself. 'Growing up all alone in that stuffy old college, with nothing but stuffy old men and grubby servants – not a proper family at all. It's not right.' She regarded Lyra with affection. 'I'm so glad I found you.'

'Yeah, me too…' said Lyra. Although clearly wary, she seemed willing to trust her new benefactress.

'Sleep well, my dear,' Mrs Coulter said. 'We've got a busy day tomorrow.' And with that, she put out the light.

As soon as the door closed behind them, the Golden Monkey and Mrs Coulter began to talk about what the dæmon had overheard. Soon they had a plan of action. It was time for the Golden Monkey to get his paws on Lyra's mysterious prize...

CHAPTER FIVE

*T*he first few days that Lyra and Pan spent with Mrs Coulter were a whirlwind of excitement. The scruffy, awkward girl from Oxford was shown the very best that London had to offer.

She was taken to the finest fashion houses, where seamstresses whisked away her old, worn clothes and dressed her up in the newest, most fashionable silks.

She dined in the best restaurants, eating out with elegant Londoners, lavishly bearded explorers and even a high-powered Magisterial official wearing a heavy chain, on which dangled an ornate seal. Mrs Coulter was utterly at home while attending these grand occasions, charming everyone with her stories and sipping casually from long-stemmed glasses of wine.

The Golden Monkey noticed that Lyra tried her best to copy Mrs Coulter by talking confidently to anyone who would listen and tentatively lifting a wine glass to her lips. He sniggered unkindly when she spat a mouthful of wine back into her glass and screwed up her face in disgust at the taste.

Pantalaimon – in the form of a frog – watched disapprovingly from nearby. Lyra responded to his unspoken criticism with a defiant, haughty look.

On another occasion, Mrs Coulter and Lyra went to a beauty salon, where an army of therapists pampered them thoroughly.

And throughout it all, Lyra was entranced by everything, gazing in amazement at the wonderful experiences she was having in her new life with Mrs Coulter.

One evening, they returned to the luxurious apartment from yet another restaurant. They stood in the living room, allowing the impeccably behaved servants to help them out of their coats.

'I *do* enjoy the Claridge,' said Mrs Coulter wistfully, 'but why they don't offer more ice for the drinks I shall never understand. Parsimonious isn't the word...'

'No, it isn't,' agreed Lyra doubtfully, as if she didn't have the foggiest idea what 'parsimonious' meant, but knew that if Mrs Coulter said it, then it must be right. She seemed totally in awe of the beautiful woman. The Golden Monkey didn't blame her one bit. It was the one sign of good taste the girl had shown.

'Perhaps I shouldn't have invited Professor Docker...?' mused her hostess. 'He's such a bore, isn't he?'

'He had sauce in his beard,' said Lyra

bluntly. 'It was the same bit of sauce as the day before.' She and Mrs Coulter shared an amused smile.

'But he is one of the foremost experts on particle metaphysics,' the elegant woman went on. 'Have I taught you what a particle is?'

'Oh, I know about particles,' said Lyra breezily, as if she answered questions like this every day of the week. 'Like Dust. That's a particle, isn't it?'

At the mention of Dust, Mrs Coulter froze and the Golden Monkey snapped its head to attention.

'Dust?' asked Mrs Coulter quickly.

Lyra nodded. 'Yeah, you know—'

'Yes!' the woman corrected her crossly.

'Sorry, yes,' Lyra said meekly. 'I mean

the Dust from space. That Dust. Like in the North.'

'And where did you hear that?' hissed Mrs Coulter.

Suddenly, Lyra no longer looked so full of confidence. 'Why?' she asked nervously. 'Did I get it wrong?'

'Answer me.'

Mrs Coulter's voice was as hard and cold as steel.

'It must've been one of the scholars at Jordan... Why, did I get it wrong?' repeated Lyra.

The Golden Monkey felt rather than saw Mrs Coulter relax as they listened to the puzzled girl. The relationship was the same for all dæmons – they always knew what their human was feeling.

When Mrs Coulter spoke again, she had regained her queenly poise. 'A wise person, Lyra, knows that there are some things it's best to ignore,' she said smoothly. 'Subjects we don't speak of.'

Lyra rushed to apologize. 'But I didn't—'

'Yes,' Mrs Coulter cut in briskly, 'you didn't know, so I forgive you. We shan't mention this again. Now, Lyra, will you please take off that childish shoulder bag. I don't like to see you wearing it indoors.'

Lyra looked down at the little leather satchel the Master had given her and the sharp-eyed Golden Monkey knew that she was thinking of the alethiometer inside. His paws itched to touch it.

'Oh, please,' pleaded Lyra. 'I do love it—'

'But I do not,' snapped Mrs Coulter. 'Put it away.'

'I don't want to,' said Lyra.

It appeared that they were as stubborn as each other. But the Golden Monkey knew that Mrs Coulter would always win in a battle of wills.

'If you do not obey me,' said Mrs Coulter ominously, 'we will have an argument, which I will win. Now, put it away at once. It looks absurd to be carrying a shoulder bag in your own home.'

At this, Lyra stiffened, while Pantalaimon turned into a polecat, arched his back and hissed loudly. 'Jordan is my home,' she said.

The Golden Monkey was as angry as Mrs Coulter. As quick as a flash, he scampered over to the polecat dæmon and overpowered him in an instant. His paw was on Pantalaimon's neck, forcing him to the ground.

Meanwhile, Mrs Coulter grabbed Lyra by

the wrist. 'You'd find Jordan much changed, dear,' she said. 'Your place is with me now.'

While Mrs Coulter spoke, the Golden Monkey pulled the girl's dæmon further and further away from her.

Held in an iron grip, Lyra couldn't move an inch. 'Don't!' she cried in pain. 'Please, it hurts... Stop pulling us apart!' It was the worst feeling in the world to be separated from her beloved dæmon. An invisible bond of energy connected humans with their dæmons, allowing them to share each other's feelings and sensations. And the further Pan and Lyra were pulled apart, the more it hurt them both.

Mrs Coulter leaned close. 'Do as I tell you, then!'

'I promise!' sobbed Lyra. All her stubbornness had vanished, like icicles in the sun.

Immediately, the Golden Monkey let go of Pantalaimon, who leapt into the girl's arms. She hugged him to her, stroking the trembling dæmon and kissing him tenderly.

'Thank you,' said Mrs Coulter. 'And while you're at it, you must learn to control your dæmon. He's much too wild.' She took a deep breath and became the calm, composed hostess once more, fully in control of her emotions. 'Now, kiss me.' And she offered a smooth cheek to Lyra, who had no choice but to obey. 'Go on and wash your face, and then we'll look through the invitations for next week,' she went on, almost as if nothing had happened. 'I'm sure there's someone we've forgotten...'

And, with that, Mrs Coulter and her dæmon were gone.

CHAPTER SIX

*T*he Golden Monkey was snooping again.

   With feather-light footsteps, he crept along the corridor and pressed an eye to the gap beneath Lyra's door. He couldn't see much, only that the girl and her dæmon were sitting on her bed. She was probably returning her mysterious device to a secret hiding place in her room. Ha! As if *that* would stop the Monkey from finding it.

'Look!' warned Pantalaimon.

Lyra swivelled and looked towards the Monkey. Hissing, 'I hate him!' she hurled her precious leather satchel at the door.

Furious that he'd let her spot his shadow, the Golden Monkey retreated to the other side of the corridor. He didn't have to see the nasty little girl in order to eavesdrop – he could hear well enough from here.

'I'll fight him… I'll beat him!' Pantalaimon said passionately.

'I hate them *both*!' cried Lyra. 'What do they want with us? Why are we here?'

'Did you see her dæmon?' said Pantalaimon 'He went all sharp when you mentioned Dust.'

The Golden Monkey tutted to himself dismissively. Very clever. So the girl and her dæmon had worked it out that Dust was important. Well, they were going to have to try a lot harder if they expected to find out what was going on. And he was hardly about to tell them.

***

Later that evening, Lyra and Pantalaimon began their investigation, with the Golden Monkey hot on their heels.

Slowly, they crept into Mrs Coulter's inner sanctum – a place so private that it hadn't featured on the tour of the house. It was a tastefully decorated room, but at night the streaks of sickly light and shadow cast by the streetlamps outside made it look very sinister.

Lyra shuddered when she saw a stylish portrait of Mrs Coulter and the Golden Monkey hanging above a large desk. Then she quickly slid open the main drawer of the desk, raking through the contents with eager hands.

Pantalaimon became an ermine and dived into the wastebasket, rustling around in the rubbish it contained. Suddenly, he poked out his white, furry head and whispered, 'Look!'

Eagerly, Lyra took the sheaf of papers from her dæmon and looked at them. Then her shoulders sank with disappointment. 'That's just one of her stupid guest lists,' she said.

'No, it isn't,' said Pantalaimon firmly.

So Lyra looked again. 'Intercision…' she read slowly. 'What does it mean, Pan?' She pointed at the top of one sheet. 'And that – General Oblation Board. What's that?'

'G.O.B…' Pan spelt out the initials in hushed tones.

'Gobblers!' Lyra exclaimed. 'From the letters G.O.B. And her…' She looked at the bottom of one sheet.

The Golden Monkey had seen the forms often enough to know what it said. AUTHORIZED: COULTER.

To Lyra, it all became clear.

'Pan! It's her – she's runnin' the Gobblers!'

The Gobblers was the name that people had given to a group of sinister individuals who were kidnapping children from the streets.

Many children had disappeared in Oxford, and Lyra had feared that she too might be abducted. The victims of the Gobblers vanished, never to be seen again. Now it seemed that Mrs Coulter was the person responsible for it all.

Lyra's shocked whisper was loud enough to wake the dead.

It was certainly loud enough to alert Mrs Coulter. 'Lyra?' she called. 'Lyra, dear?'

The girl rushed from the room and was standing guiltily in the corridor when her benefactress appeared.

Silently, the Golden Monkey shared a glance with Mrs Coulter and slipped away. He had work to do.

'Lyra, dear… What have you been doing?' said Mrs Coulter, in her honeyed tones. She spoke as if their earlier confrontation had never happened.

'Nothin',' muttered Lyra.

'Nothing?' repeated Mrs Coulter. Her voice was pleasant, but firm. 'Well … then we must find something for you to do. Shall you help me arrange our passage to Norroway?' She beckoned at Lyra with an elegant, carefully manicured finger.

Lyra hesitated.

'You do want to come to the North with me, don't you?' asked Mrs Coulter softly.

The Golden Monkey chuckled to himself as he heard the conversation swing back and forth. He padded along the corridor that led to Lyra's room and, as the distant voices rumbled on, pushed open the door and silently closed it behind him. He surveyed the sea of dazzling white and pink.

Suddenly a flash of inspiration hit him. The bed. That's where it was.

With a great leap, he rocketed through the air and landed on the luxurious eiderdown. Quickly, he scampered to the pillow and delved a tiny paw beneath it. He touched leather almost immediately.

He had it!

The Golden Monkey slid the small leather satchel from beneath the pillow and drew out the mysterious, compass-like object he had heard Lyra and her dæmon talking about. So this is the alethiometer, he thought, and stroked it gently. Up close, it was more amazing than he could ever have imagined.

Thirty-six symbols ringed the face of the compass-like device – ant, hourglass, skull, dolphin, anchor, chameleon, bull, beehive… And as Lyra had said, a needle swung around the face of its own accord. Three more hands pointed outwards. There were also dials on the edge of the object – when the Golden Monkey twisted them, the hands moved.

The dæmon had never seen anything so beautiful, so complex and so magical.

Suddenly, Pantalaimon's voice wailed through the house like an annoying siren. 'Where is *he*? I don't see him!'

The Golden Monkey shrugged. So the dæmon and the girl had discovered they'd been tricked. So what? He had the alethiometer now. And soon it would belong to Mrs Coulter.

Furious footsteps thudded along the corridor and the door swung open, rebounding against the wall with a noisy crash. Lyra and her dæmon stood there, shaking with anger.

'No!' roared the girl.

The Monkey hissed at them.

But he hadn't counted on Pantalaimon. The girl's dæmon leapt into the form of a bird and flew past the Golden Monkey, plucking the alethiometer from his grasp and soaring out of the window. With a look of triumph, Lyra followed, hopping through the gap and into the blackness beyond.

The Golden Monkey scampered after them. He sprang on to the sill, ready to hurl himself into the night to win back the alethiometer for his beloved Mrs Coulter.

Crash!

The window smashed down on to his paw, sending waves of pain shooting through him. The girl had not vanished after all, but lain in wait. Now the Golden Monkey was the one to be tricked. He yelped in agony.

'Lyra!' Mrs Coulter burst through the doorway, looking in dismay at the empty room and her injured dæmon. She was holding her own hand awkwardly, and the Golden Monkey knew Mrs Coulter was feeling the same pain as him.

Angrily, the creature peered through the window into the darkness. Even if he wanted to, he couldn't follow... the Monkey couldn't tear himself so far away from Mrs Coulter. However much it hurt the Golden Monkey to admit it, his enemies and the precious alethiometer were gone.

Lyra, Pantalaimon and their glittering prize were safe, for now...

GLOSSARY

The world of the Golden Compass is a world very much like ours, in a parallel universe. Much of it would be familiar to us – the continents, the oceans, Brytain, Norroway and the North Pole ... but much is shockingly different. On this parallel Earth, a person's soul lives on the outside of their body, in the form of a dæmon – a talking animal spirit that accompanies them through life. A child's dæmon can change shape, assuming all the forms that a child's infinite potential inspires; but as a person ages, their dæmon gradually settles into one form, according to their character and nature.

CHARACTERS

Lyra

Lyra Belacqua is a twelve-year-old girl who has been left by her Uncle Asriel to be raised by the scholars and fellows of Jordan College in Oxford, Brytain. Headstrong, rebellious and wilful, Lyra's carefree existence comes to an end after numerous children, including her friend Roger, mysteriously begin to disappear. Lyra's dæmon is Pantalaimon (Pan).

Mrs Coulter

Strikingly glamorous – yet mysteriously sinister – Mrs Coulter is a beautiful, powerful woman who takes a particular interest in Lyra. Her mysterious aims are in some way tied in with Lyra's very fate. Mrs Coulter's dæmon is a nameless Golden Monkey.

Roger Parslow

The Jordan College kitchen boy who is Lyra's best friend and playmate. The more cautious of the two, Roger's abduction sets in motion a string of events that thrusts Lyra on a perilous journey to fulfil her destiny. Roger's dæmon is Salcilia.

The Gobblers

A sinister band of kidnappers rumoured to be prowling the streets of London and now Oxford. They abduct the children of the poor and the marginalized – orphans, servant children, Gyptians – and take them North, for unknown purposes.

❧——————————— DEFINITIONS ———————————☙

Alethiometer

Also known as the Golden Compass, the alethiometer is an extraordinarily intricate device that was made in the sixteenth century. Its needle seeks out, instead of true North, Truth itself. The ornamented face of the device is divided into 36 symbols, each of which may convey different meanings in combination with any of the others and according to the subtleties of the machine's motions. Reading the alethiometer is a difficult task, but Lyra Belacqua possesses a natural ability to use the instrument.

Jordan College

Jordan College is the oldest, richest and grandest of the colleges of Oxford in Lyra's world. A bastion of critical inquiry, scholarship and free thought, the college often runs afoul of the oppressive Magisterium. Jordan has been Lyra's unlikely home since infancy, and her childhood has been spent prowling the roofs and rattling through the streets of Oxford, much to the dismay of the fellows and servants of the college.

The Magisterium

The powerful organization that dominates the politics and society of Lyra's world, in Brytain and beyond. It has established a ruthless, iron-grip on the nations of the world.

There are worlds beyond our own
— the Compass will show the way ...

Read all three books and follow the exciting
adventures of Pan, Iorek and the Golden Monkey!

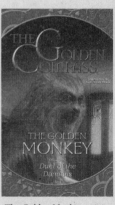

Pan and the
Prisoners of Bolvangar

Iorek and the
Gyptian Alliance

The Golden Monkey and the
Duel of the Dæmons